NEVER Let a DIPLODOCUS Draw

For Mummy and Baba. With love.
R.S.

For the artist in each and every one of us (Dippy included)
D.E.

PUFFIN BOOKS

UK | USA | Canada | Ireland | Australia | India | New Zealand | South Africa

Puffin Books is part of the Penguin Random House group of companies
whose addresses can be found at global.penguinrandomhouse.com.

Penguin
Random House
UK

First published 2022
001

Text copyright © Rashmi Sirdeshpande, 2022
Illustrations copyright © Diane Ewen, 2022
The moral right of the author and illustrator has been asserted

Printed and bound in Italy

The authorized representative in the EEA is Penguin Random House Ireland,
Morrison Chambers, 32 Nassau Street, Dublin D02 YH68

A CIP catalogue record for this book is available from the British Library

ISBN: 978–0–241–56251–2

All correspondence to: Puffin Books, Penguin Random House Children's
One Embassy Gardens, 8 Viaduct Gardens, London SW11 7BW

MIX
Paper from
responsible sources
FSC® C018179
FSC
www.fsc.org

NEVER Let a DIPLODOCUS Draw

Rashmi Sirdeshpande & **Diane Ewen**

PUFFIN

NEVER
let a **Diplodocus**
draw a picture.

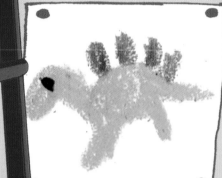

Do you have ANY idea what might happen if you do?

She'll start with pencils and crayons.

Other way round, Dippy! There you go!

Then maybe she'll try a **splash** of paint.

OOPS. OK, maybe a little less paint.

She's going to love all the
stamping and **printing** . . .

. . . and **cutting** and **sticking**.

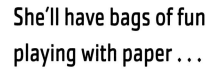

She'll have bags of fun
playing with paper . . .

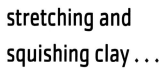

stretching and
squishing clay . . .

and making models out of
old cereal boxes and cartons!

And if you give her a bit of glue and newspaper strips,
she'll come up with all sorts of **interesting** creations!

You'll have to introduce Dippy to some other artists!
She'll love that. They're sure to spark some ideas.

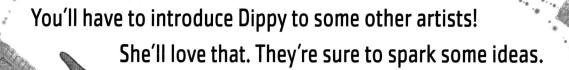

She'll want to figure out her own style too.
That might take a few attempts.

SCRUNCH

SCRUNCH

SCRUNNNNNCH!

And when she gets it JUST how she wants it . . .

she'll be so happy that you might even
get a big, squishy dino hug!

AWWWWW!

But just you wait until . . .

. . . someone DISCOVERS her work.
Because if that happens they'll be so excited,
they'll tell everyone they know.

And **THEY** will tell everyone **THEY** know . . .

PRICELESS MASTERPIECE

SECURITY

GALLERY

Until **EVERYONE** is talking about her.

The news is bound to reach the local art gallery.

And if it does . . . WELL . . .

. . . they're going to want to put her work on display!
You just know it's going to be a huge hit because
LOOK AT IT.

And if it's a hit, then ALL the big galleries will want her amazing artwork.

THEN they'll be selling her paintings in the fanciest places.
(For a lot of money too!)

"Going once!
     Going twice!

SOLD to the triceratops
        in the blue bandana for
             **TWO GAZILLION
                  POUNDS!**"

Crispy's
Auction House

And that's just the beginning . . .

Town mayors will ask her
to make **dinormous**
sculptures and paint
whole buildings.

Famous Artist
in Town

TOWN HALL

In which case, she might need
a bit more paint.

People will love her art SO much that they'll want it in their homes too.

CHECK OUT
THAT
FANCY
WALLPAPER!

Dippy Designs

And look at Dippy's **CLOTHES!**

Movie stars will want to wear her latest designs.
So you'll have to fly Dippy over to Hollywood!

I ♥ Dippy

And what do you suppose will happen then?

She'll be SO FAMOUS that her fantastic artwork and her gorgeous face will be

EVERYWHERE!

On bags . . .

toys . . .

and cakes too!

How about THAT?

Dippy will be such a superstar, EVERYONE is going to want to paint like her. And they can! Because Dippy is going to hold the **BIGGEST EVER ART CLASS IN THE WHOLE WIDE WORLD.**

Imagine that! Lots of fun and LOTS of painting!
The only trouble is, lots of painting means
lots of PAINT . . .

and do you know
what that means???

PAINT FACTORY

YIKES!!!

The paint factory doesn't look like it'll hold much longer . . .

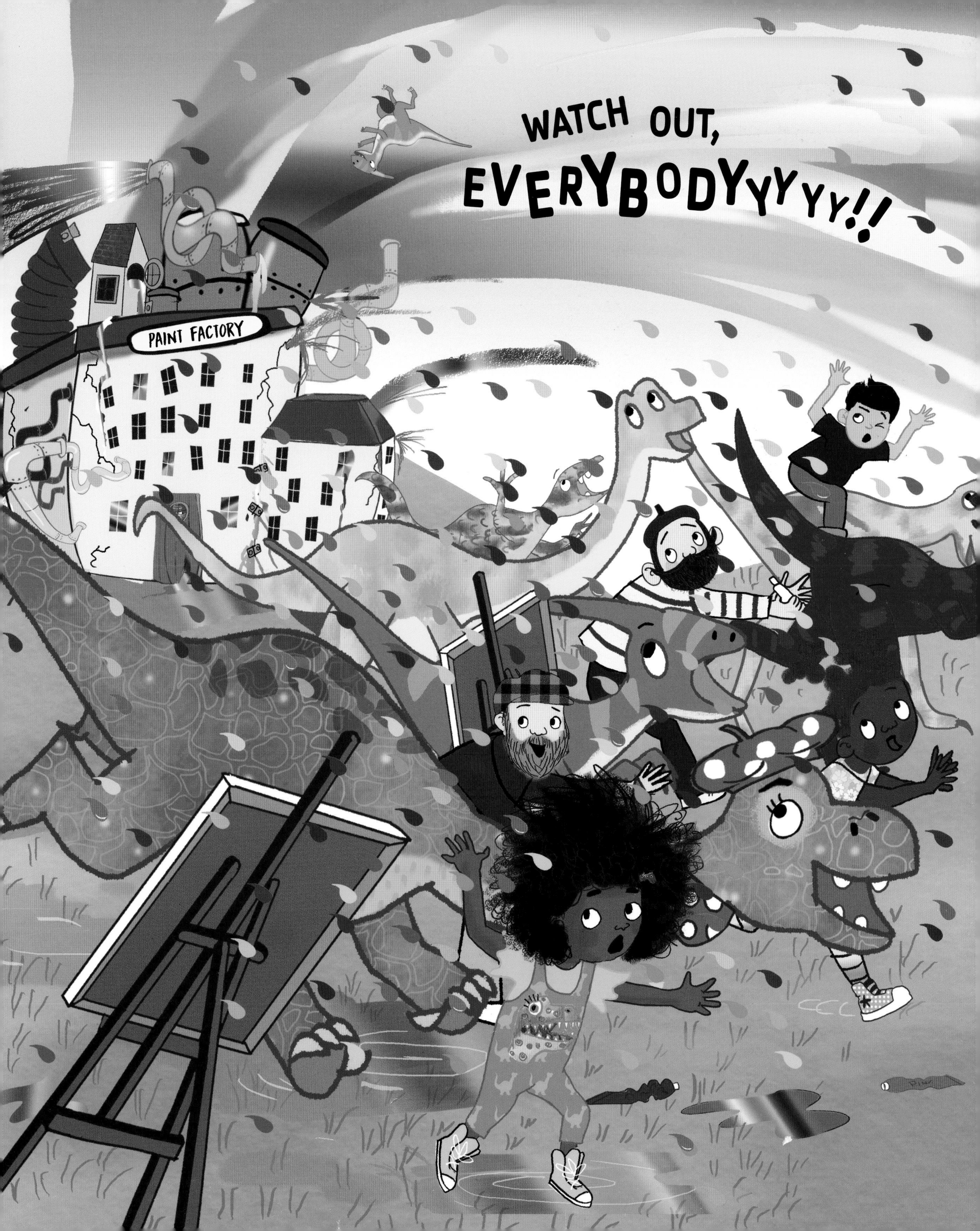

WATCH OUT,

EVERYBODYYYYY!!

Oh no . . .
How will you be able
to do art now?

Still, you should probably
clean up . . .

Time to get the hose out!

THERE WE GO! All washed up.
Better pop those paintings up to dry too.
You wouldn't want to lose any of them.